Sept 16, 2002

To Kay Daniels, WGM, on
her Grand Visitation to Unity #112.
This is dedicated to the "youngster"
in all of us.   Judith Harrison, WM
             Ernest Buckhead, WP

NOAH'S SQUARE DANCE

RICK WALTON 🐟 **THOR WICKSTROM**

LOTHROP, LEE & SHEPARD BOOKS   NEW YORK

To Mom and Dad, who did their best to keep their animals from drowning—RW

For Eric, Linda, and Trevor—TW

Library of Congress Cataloging in Publication Data
Walton, Rick. Noah's square dance / by Rick Walton ; illustrated by Thor Wickstrom.
p.   cm. Summary: As Noah calls, the animals on the ark perform a variety of square dance steps.
ISBN 0-688-11186-6. — ISBN 0-688-11187-4 (lib. bdg.).[1. Noah's ark—Fiction.
2. Square dancing—Fiction. 3. Animals—Fiction. 4. Stories in rhyme.] I. Wickstrom, Thor, ill.
II. Title. PZ8.3.W199No 1993 [E]—dc20 92-10257 CIP AC

All night rain pounds on Noah's Ark,
But candles chase away the dark
As fiddlers rosin up their bows
And dancers start to tap their toes.
Noah begins:

The stalls are scrubbed, your chores are done—
Now it's time to have some fun.

So pick your partners and form a square,
Then bow and curtsey, pair by pair.

Do-si-do your corners all!
Walk or waddle, hop or crawl.

Now allemande left and everybody chain—
Let your feet keep beat with the pourin' rain.

Around the ark march two by two.
Stop to wheel that caribou.

Skip down the center and split the ring.
Now grab ahold of a turkey wing.

Separate now, four in a line—
Don't get too close to the porcupine.

Circle once, then twirl that lion.
Lizards, keep those petticoats flyin'!

Now a right-and-left grand and away you go.
Come on, now, skunk, don't be so slow!

Pick up your honey with a left arm 'round
And swing that hippo off the ground.

Listen!
Hear it?
NO MORE DROPS!
HALLELUJAH!—THE STORM HAS STOPPED!

Off to the right and circle four,
Then run to the center and everyone

ROAR!